An Owl Called Star

HELEN PETERS

illustrated by
ELLIE SNOWDON

nosy
crow

HELEN PETERS

For Orlando and Noah
H. P.

For Clo
E. S.

First published in the UK in 2019 by Nosy Crow Ltd
The Crow's Nest, 14 Baden Place,
Crosby Row, London SE1 1YW, UK

Nosy Crow and associated logos are trademarks and/or registered
trademarks of Nosy Crow Ltd

Text copyright © Helen Peters, 2019
Cover and illustrations copyright © Ellie Snowdon, 2019

The right of Helen Peters and Ellie Snowdon to be identified
as the author and illustrator respectively of this work has been asserted
by them in accordance with the Copyright, Designs
and Patents Act 1988.

A CIP catalogue record for this book will be available from the British Library.

Printed and bound in Great Britain by Clays Ltd, Elcograf S.p.A.

Papers used by Nosy Crow are made from wood grown in
sustainable forests.

  ISBN: 978 1 78800 478 7

www.nosycrow.com

Chapter One
A Perfect Place for a Party

"I can't believe my parents won't let us have a Halloween party," said Jasmine to her best friend, Tom. "They promised! How can they just go back on their word like that?"

It was a Thursday evening just before October half term, and they were taking Jasmine's sheepdog, Sky, for a walk in the woods at the edge of Jasmine's farm.

"Did they definitely say no?" asked Tom.

"Completely. Mum denied she'd even promised us. She said she didn't remember

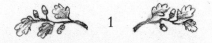

1

anything about it and she's far too busy. And then Dad started going on about how the house still hadn't recovered from Manu's birthday."

"But that's not your fault," said Tom.

"Exactly! I wasn't the one who spilled food colouring all over the carpet or set fire to the dolls' house."

Tom shook his head in sympathy. "It's so unfair."

"I don't suppose there's any chance of having it at yours?" asked Jasmine hopefully.

Tom snorted. "No chance, sorry. Mum said she's got enough to do without a load of marauding children all over the house."

Jasmine kicked at a pile of crunchy autumn leaves with her wellington boot, scattering twigs and nuts across the narrow path.

The wood at the edge of Oak Tree Farm was Jasmine's favourite place. It was especially lovely at this time of year, when the leaf-littered ground was scattered with shiny ripe conkers and little brown acorns. Fat purple sloes and gleaming

2

red holly berries lent splashes of colour to the autumn hedgerows, and mysterious toadstools sprouted up among the mossy tree roots.

Sky was enjoying the walk too. His feathery tail wagged happily as he trotted up the path ahead of the children, darting in and out of the woods to sniff at piles of leaves and investigate rabbit holes. Now he disappeared into a clump of trees away to their right.

"Sky!" called Jasmine, when he didn't reappear.

Sky didn't come. They carried on walking for a minute and then Jasmine called him again.

They heard leaves rustling and twigs snapping. He was clearly having a lovely time.

"He's pretending to be deaf," said Jasmine. "Let's go and find him."

Away from the path, the woodland floor was a tangle of bracken and brambles. Jasmine and Tom gingerly stepped through the waist-high undergrowth, treading down the brambles and trying not to snag their jeans on thorns.

They were close to the edge of the wood now, where the landscape opened out into fields that ran all the way to the South Downs. The sun was setting behind the hills in a blaze of red. In the wood, the light was becoming grey and shadowy.

"I wonder if he's in that old barn over there," said Tom.

There was a tumbledown barn in a field at the edge of the woods. It wasn't part of Jasmine's farm, but belonged to somebody else. It looked as though it had been abandoned for a hundred years. There were great gaps in the walls where the wooden planks had rotted away or were hanging off at crazy angles. The tiled roof sagged in the middle and some of the tiles had slipped off, leaving jagged holes. The walls were covered in ivy, and the ground around the barn was overgrown with nettles, brambles and scrubby bushes.

Tom and Jasmine climbed over the fence at the edge of the wood and walked towards the barn.

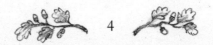

Suddenly,
from somewhere
overhead, came
a loud, spooky,
screeching sound.
The children
jumped in shock.

"What was *that*?" whispered Tom.

Jasmine gasped and pointed out into the field. "Look!"

A barn owl was flying towards them, ghostly white in the twilight. It swooped silently over their heads and vanished into the shadowy trees.

"Wow," said Tom, when the owl was out of sight. "That was amazing."

"So cool," said Jasmine. "I've never seen one before. Its wings didn't make a sound, did they?"

"It must be hunting," said Tom. "Do you think it was the owl making that screeching sound?"

"Yes," said Jasmine. "I've heard it before, and Dad said it was a barn owl."

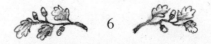

They had reached the old barn now.

"Sky!" called Jasmine.

There was a scuffling sound from inside, and then Sky bounded out, wagging his tail happily.

"Good dog," said Jasmine, ruffling his soft furry coat.

Tom was gazing through the barn doorway. "Look at this. Have you ever been inside?"

"No," she said, stroking Sky's silky ears. "It's probably full of rats."

Jasmine loved all animals, but a barn full of rats wasn't a tempting thought.

"Come and look," said Tom.

Jasmine stepped through the undergrowth to join him, followed by Sky.

The barn was completely empty. The dirt floor was covered in animal and bird droppings. Enormous rough beams held up the roof and ran across the width of the building. In the one window, Jasmine was surprised to see the glass was still intact.

She gazed at the dim empty space, and all at once she wasn't just seeing the inside of a dirty old barn. In her mind's eye, she saw glowing pumpkin lanterns; decorations strung from the beams; Halloween-themed cupcakes; biscuits in the shapes of cats and owls.

She turned to Tom, excitement bubbling up inside her.

"Tom!" she said. "Wouldn't this be an amazing place for a Halloween party?"

Tom's eyes widened.

"It would be *perfect*. But it's not our barn."

"So? The owner lives in London. He doesn't care about it."

"But our parents will never let us."

"No," said Jasmine. "They'll never let us. So we'll just have to have the party in secret. Won't we?"

Chapter Two

Something
In the Brambles

"How can we have a Halloween party without anyone finding out?" said Tom.

"We just tell everyone not to tell their parents."

"But won't their parents want to know where they're going?"

Jasmine thought for a second. "I know! We'll tell them all to meet at your house to go trick-or-treating. Then we'll just walk here instead. It will be a great spooky start to Halloween, walking from your house through the woods. We can tell ghost stories on the way."

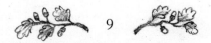

"What about my parents, though, when everyone turns up at my house?"

Jasmine screwed up her mouth in thought. "Can you get them to go out? They like going to the cinema, don't they?"

"I could tell them I'm going to be with you for Halloween," said Tom. "Which won't be a lie. So then they'll have the evening free to go out."

Jasmine stepped inside the barn. "We can make paper bats and spiders and hang them from the beams. It will look so good."

"We'll never reach those beams," said Tom. "And we can't carry a ladder all the way here."

Jasmine thought quickly. "So we'll tie a decoration on to each end of a long piece of string and then throw the string over the beam. We can make loads of them. And we can have fairy lights too."

"There's no electricity to plug in fairy lights," said Tom.

Jasmine rolled her eyes. "Honestly, are you

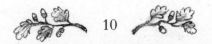

just trying to find problems? We've got fairy lights with batteries. Mum puts them on the mantelpiece at Christmas. And we can make cupcakes and biscuits and popcorn. It will be amazing."

"It will be amazing if it works," said Tom.

Sky ran out of the barn and started bounding across the field.

"He's heading home," said Jasmine. "Shall we go? It's nearly dark."

Standing in the doorway, Jasmine glimpsed something white in the brambles outside. She tutted.

"Look, a plastic bag. Why are people so horrible? Don't they know animals can die from eating litter?"

She picked her way through the undergrowth towards it. Jasmine was constantly coming home with her pockets full of other people's rubbish. She couldn't bear to think of an animal suffocating inside a bag, or choking on a piece of

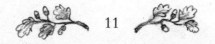

plastic they'd mistaken for food.

As she drew closer, though, and saw the patch of white more clearly, she realised it wasn't plastic after all.

"Feathers! Oh, no, it's a dead bird."

"Oh, that's so sad," said Tom.

Jasmine made her way to the bird and crouched down.

She gasped. "Look!"

Tom hurried towards her. He drew in his breath. "A barn owl!"

The owl lay motionless on its side amongst the dead leaves. It had a beautiful white heart-shaped face and a white chest. Its head and wings were light brown and grey, speckled with black-and-white dots. Its eyes were closed.

"It might still be alive," said Tom. "Let's check."

Trying to avoid the thorns, they moved the brambles out of the way. Jasmine wriggled her hand through the gap and felt through the bird's outer feathers to the soft down beneath.

12

"It's warm!" she said, her heart beating faster with excitement. "But we need to get it home quickly. I'll wrap it in my coat."

"I wonder what happened to it," said Tom. "Do you think it will be all right?"

There was a rustling in the undergrowth as Sky ran back towards them, head down, sniffing the ground. He barged past Tom, heading straight for the owl. Tom grabbed his collar.

"Oh, no, you don't. Come away, Sky. Have you got his lead, Jasmine?"

Jasmine took Sky's lead out of her coat pocket and handed it to Tom. Then she took off her coat and spread it on the ground. Cautiously, she scooped up the bird.

"It's so light! It weighs practically nothing. I wonder how long it's been here."

She wrapped the owl in her coat so that only its face was showing. Then she picked it up and held it close to her chest.

"Be careful of its beak," said Tom. "If it wakes up, it might peck you."

Jasmine turned the bundled-up owl around so it was facing outwards, and moved her hands further away from the beak.

"I hope Mum's at home," she said, as they hurried across the darkening field.

"Has she ever treated a barn owl?" asked Tom.

"I don't know. But she loves owls, so she knows a lot about them."

 14

Jasmine's mum, Nadia, was a vet, and she had helped Jasmine and Tom to look after other animals they had rescued. It was hard to imagine now, but Sky had once been desperately in need of emergency care. Jasmine had found him under a hedge as a puppy, abandoned and starving, and had nursed him back to health. She had also rescued a tiny runt piglet, an egg that had hatched into a duckling, a kitten, a lamb, two sparrow chicks, a baby goat and an otter cub. But she had never brought home an owl before.

"What shall we call it?" she asked.

"What about Barney?" said Tom. "Since it's a barn owl?"

"I think it should be something more mysterious. Something to do with night."

"Shadow?" suggested Tom. "Moonlight?"

"Moonlight's nice," said Jasmine. "He's pale like moonlight."

"Or Starlight?" said Tom, looking up at the night sky.

"Star!" said Jasmine. "Just Star. That's perfect."

She smiled at the owl. But Tom had a worried frown on his face.

"Do you really think it's alive?" he said. "It's so still."

"It was warm," said Jasmine. "I told you."

"I know, but… Well, if it had died recently, it might still be warm, mightn't it?"

Jasmine felt tense with anxiety, and the fear made her cross.

"What's the point of saying that? We just have to get home as fast as we can. I can't walk any quicker and I'm not going to run in case I jolt the owl and injure it."

"I know," said Tom. "Sorry. I was just worried."

"I'm worried too. But we're doing all we can. We'll just have to hope it's not too late."

Chapter Three
We Need to Work Quickly

As they approached the farmyard, Jasmine saw her mum standing by the car boot, rummaging through her box of vets' equipment.

Jasmine hurried towards her. "You're not going out, are you?"

"Afraid so," said Nadia. "I've got to go and see a cow at Foxheath Farm."

"You can't."

"Why not?"

"Because of this."

Jasmine held out the coat so her mum could

see Star's beautiful face.

"Oh, my goodness," said Nadia. "Where did you find a barn owl?"

"Lying in some brambles by the wood. It hasn't moved at all. And it's so light, Mum." Jasmine felt tears coming to her eyes. She blinked them away. "I think it must be starving."

"Jasmine," said Nadia gently, putting her hand on her daughter's arm. "Are you sure this owl is…?"

"Alive? It was warm when I picked it up. But we need to be quick, don't we? Can't someone else go and look at the cow?"

Mum nodded. "You're right, we need to examine the owl straightaway." She took her phone from her pocket. "I'll ring David and see if he can go to Foxheath."

David was Nadia's partner at the vet's surgery. Jasmine and Tom waited anxiously while Nadia told him about the owl. They couldn't make out his reply, but finally Nadia said, "Oh, thank you so much, David. You're an absolute star."

She put the phone back in her pocket. "Right," she said. "Let's have a look at this owl."

★⋆

Inside the farmhouse, Jasmine's seventeen-year-old sister, Ella, was doing her homework at the kitchen table. As usual, she had spread her books

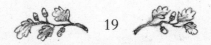

19

and papers over the entire surface. Jasmine's ginger cat, Toffee, was sitting on Ella's lap. Her black cat, Marmite, was curled up on a chair. Manu, Jasmine's seven-year-old brother, was sprawled on the tiled floor, taking a toy car to pieces with a screwdriver.

Manu looked up as Jasmine, Tom and Nadia walked into the room. His eyes widened as he saw the bird wrapped in Jasmine's coat.

"An owl! Cool! Where did you find it?" He scrambled to his feet and peered at Star's face. "Is it dead?"

Jasmine turned away from him and held the owl closer. "No, but it needs peace and quiet, so don't come near. It's called Star."

"It's so beautiful," said Ella. "What happened to it?"

"We don't know yet," said Nadia. "We're going to examine it."

"I thought you were going out," said Manu.

"David's going instead," said Jasmine, as they

20

walked into the scullery. "Make sure the cats don't come in here."

Nadia shut the door behind them. Then she took Jasmine's coat with the owl wrapped up inside it. She laid it on the worktop and opened out the coat.

"There's no smell," she said, "which is a good sign. That should mean he doesn't have an infected injury. And he's not bleeding."

"How do you know it's a boy?" asked Jasmine.

"See how his throat and chest are pure white? Females have a pale brown throat, and their chests are spotted. Jasmine, can you hold him while I examine him?"

"Yes, please," said Jasmine.

"Sorry, Tom," said Mum, "but barn owls can do a lot of damage with their feet in particular, and if he does scratch or peck, I'd rather he injured Jasmine than you."

"Wow, thanks," said Jasmine.

Nadia smiled. "Not that you will get injured if

you hold him properly. The main thing is to keep
control of his feet. And put a pair of gloves on."

Jasmine took her gloves from her coat pockets.

"Hold him close to your chest," said Nadia,
"with your left arm around his body, so you're
keeping his wings under control, and hold his
legs with your right hand. Make sure you've got
his feet pointing away from you, then he won't
be able to hurt you if he does start to struggle."

She picked up the owl and handed him to
Jasmine.

"He weighs nothing, doesn't he?" said Jasmine.
"Do you think he's starving?"

"We'll check now," said Mum. "Even healthy
barn owls are surprisingly light, though. They're
mostly feathers. That's one reason why they can
fly so silently. Tom, can you grab a cloth from
that drawer? If he opens his eyes and starts to
struggle, lay the cloth gently over his face, and
it will calm him down. Owls are calmer in the
dark."

She ran her fingers down the centre of the bird's chest feathers. "OK," she said. "This bone in the middle of his chest is called the keel. It shouldn't stick up more than a couple of millimetres from the chest muscles on either side of it. If it sticks up more than about five millimetres, it means the bird doesn't have much chest muscle left."

She felt on both sides of the owl's chest. Then she ran her finger down to the stomach.

"The breastbone is sticking up," she said, "and his stomach is hollow. He hasn't eaten very recently."

"Poor Star," said Tom. "What do you think happened to him?"

"Maybe a broken bone," said Mum. "The most common injury in owls is broken wing bones, especially if they're young and have just left the nest."

"Do you think he's young?" asked Jasmine.

"It's likely, but impossible to tell. He's fully grown, which means he might be any age from twelve weeks upwards. Barn owls are fully grown at about twelve weeks, and then they leave the nest to find their own territory. That's when most of them get injured. Often they fly low across roads and get hit by cars."

"It can't have been a car," said Jasmine, "because he wasn't near a road."

 24

"Sometimes they fly into overhead wires," said Mum, "or into windows. They don't realise there's glass there, so they just fly straight into it and break a bone or knock themselves out."

Tom's eyes opened wide. "There was a window in the barn just above where we found him."

"Oh, yes," said Jasmine. "So maybe Star flew into it."

"If he was flying as fast as that other owl we saw," said Tom, "he must have really hurt himself."

"And if he hasn't eaten recently, that might mean he was lying on the ground for ages," said Jasmine.

"It's very lucky that you spotted him," said Mum. "If we're going to save his life, we need to work quickly."

Chapter Four
We'll Just
Have to Hope

"We'll check to see if Star has broken any bones," said Mum, "and then we'll rehydrate him. If you take your hand away there, Jasmine, I'll examine his wings."

She took hold of Star's wing and spread the feathers out like a fan.

"Wow, his wings are huge," said Jasmine.

"Their wingspan is nearly a metre," said Nadia, as she felt the bones at the top of the wing. "That's another thing that helps them fly so quietly."

"His legs are really long," said Tom. "I always

thought owls had short legs."

"Not barn owls," said Nadia, as she checked Star's other wing. "It's one of the ways they've adapted to be such good hunters. They mainly eat field voles, you see, which live in rough grass, so the owls need those legs to land in the grass and grab their prey."

Jasmine looked at Star's sharp pointed talons and shuddered. "Poor voles."

"If you let go of one leg," said Nadia, "I'll check it over. Keep hold of the other one."

She felt Star's leg bones carefully.

"They both feel good," she said, "and the feet look fine, too, so I don't think there's anything wrong with them."

"So what do we do next?" asked Jasmine.

"Tom, could you grab my laptop from my study, please?" said Mum. "We need to find out what weight he should be. And bring a pad and pen, then you can note everything down."

"It must be a bad sign that he's had his eyes

closed all this time," said Jasmine, as Tom went to fetch everything.

"Not necessarily," said Mum. "Wild barn owls often close their eyes as a reaction to shock."

Jasmine stroked the owl's feathers. "They're so soft."

"That's another thing that helps them fly so quietly," said Mum. She fetched the digital scales from the kitchen and took an empty shoebox from a cupboard. Tom appeared with the laptop.

"Thank you," said Mum. "Could you look at the Barn Owl Trust website and find out what weight he should be? While you're doing that, I'll check his head area."

She gently opened Star's left eye. It was very dark brown, almost black.

"That looks great," she said. "Very bright and healthy."

She opened the other eye.

"All good there, too. OK, let's look inside his beak."

She took hold of the upper beak and gently pulled it open.

"It's lovely and pink inside his mouth. That all looks very healthy. And his nostrils are clear."

"Where are his nostrils?" asked Jasmine.

Mum pointed to the top of the beak. "Those little holes there, see? I'm going to check his ears, too. If he's had a blow to the head, there might be some bleeding."

Star's ears didn't stick out like human ears. Mum had to part the feathers at the side of his head to reveal a little opening.

"See how his left and right ears are at slightly different heights? That means he can tell more accurately where a sound is coming from."

"That's so clever," said Jasmine.

"Barn owls have the best hearing of any animal ever tested," said Mum, as she examined the other ear. "Much better than ours. And his ears are both fine, so that's good news."

"I've found the weight chart," said Tom.

"Great," said Mum. She weighed the empty shoebox on the scales, then gently placed Star in the box. She told Tom the two weights and he did a quick calculation.

"Star weighs two hundred and thirty grams," he said.

"Is that good?" asked Jasmine.

Tom looked at the chart.

"Oh, no."

"What?" asked Jasmine, alarmed.

"Two hundred and thirty grams is starvation weight."

"Right," said Nadia. "We need to get liquid into him straightaway, or he won't survive much longer. We'll wrap him up to keep him still while we feed him. Tom, can you fetch the kettle? I boiled it a while ago, so it should be just about the right temperature."

Nadia spread out an old towel on the work surface. Jasmine carefully laid Star on it and Nadia wrapped him up. Then she smiled at Tom,

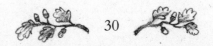

who had returned with the kettle.

"Would you like to fetch a chair and hold him while I feed him?" she asked. "He's wrapped securely so he can't do you any damage."

Tom smiled excitedly. "Sure."

"And Jasmine," said Mum, "can you mix one and a half teaspoons of glucose powder into a cup of warm water, please. I need to go to the car for a syringe and some tubing."

When she came back, Tom was sitting down, holding Star upright on his lap.

"OK," said Nadia. "You need to hold his neck very straight."

She drew up three millilitres of the glucose mixture into the syringe. Then she opened Star's beak, lifted his head slightly and lowered the tube through the corner of his mouth. She pushed the syringe plunger right down.

"There we are. We'll give him the same again in a few hours' time. He needs about ten mils a day."

"What about food?" asked Jasmine.

"We can't feed him yet," said Nadia. "He won't be able to swallow while he's dazed. We'll just have to hope he comes out of his daze soon."

The way she said it made Jasmine glance at her in alarm.

"Do you mean … he might not come out of it?"

"I honestly don't know," said Nadia. "We'll just have to hope."

The door from the kitchen opened and Manu appeared.

"When will the owl wake up?" he asked.

"Soon, hopefully," said Jasmine. "But you're not allowed anywhere near him, OK?"

"That's not fair. I'd be great with him."

"Huh," said Jasmine, who still hadn't forgiven her brother for various other incidents involving animals she'd rescued. "Great like you were with Pebble? And the kittens?"

"That was different," said Manu. "I can train this owl. I'd be a really good owl trainer."

"Wild owls can't be trained," said Tom. "It says on the website."

"What about the ones in the *Harry Potter* films?"

"They must have been bred in captivity," said Nadia.

"I bet it's really easy to train them," said Manu. "I'm going to train this one to carry letters for me, like Harry's."

"Let's put him in a box where he can rest," said Mum. "Can you fetch the pet carrier, Jasmine?"

Jasmine fetched it and laid a folded towel inside it. Nadia put on a pair of leather gloves, unwrapped Star and laid him on his side in the carrier. Jasmine covered the wire mesh doors with towels so that Star would feel calm in the dark.

"Make sure it's closed properly," Mum said. "He could start moving at any time."

"Should we put some food and drink in with him?" asked Jasmine.

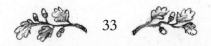

"No, there's no point. Even if he comes out of the daze, he won't eat or drink by himself yet."

"Can he go in my room? I'll be really quiet."

"All right," said Mum. "As long as you keep the cats out."

"Yay!" said Jasmine. Then she looked at Nadia suspiciously. "What happens when he wakes up? You won't make us send him to a wildlife rehabilitator, will you?"

Mum smiled. "Let's see how we go, shall we?"

Tom's mum, Mel, came to collect him soon after that.

"Can we have a sleepover here tomorrow night?" asked Jasmine. "Please, Mum? Then Tom can help feed Star."

"That's fine by me, if it's OK with Mel," said Nadia.

"Are you sure?" said Mel.

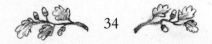

"Honestly, it's no problem," said Nadia. "It's not often he'll get to spend time close up with a barn owl."

"Well, that's very kind," said Mel.

"Promise you'll phone me if Star wakes up tonight," Tom said.

"I will," said Jasmine.

She spent the evening in her bedroom, making Halloween decorations for the barn. She cut out bat shapes from black paper and threaded them on strings. She sneaked up to the attic and rummaged in the boxes of Christmas decorations until she found the battery-operated fairy lights, which she took to her room and hid in her chest of drawers. She made a list of all the people in their class they could invite to the party, people who could be trusted to keep it a secret.

Every so often, she peeped into Star's box.

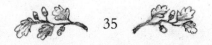

But Star was still lying on his side with his eyes closed.

Would they still be able to have the party if Star hadn't recovered?

But it would only be for a few hours, and Mum would be around to look after him.

At eight o'clock, Jasmine and Nadia fed him again.

"I'll give him another three mils at eleven," said Nadia, "and then we'll see how he is in the morning."

Jasmine knew Mum would say no if she asked to stay up for the eleven o'clock feed. So she decided not to ask. She made the party invitations, and then she set her alarm for a quarter to eleven. When it woke her, she waited in bed until Mum came in. Then she turned over, yawned, opened her eyes and sat up.

"Go back to sleep, Jasmine," Mum whispered. "I was trying not to wake you. You've got school in the morning."

"I'll just help you feed him," said Jasmine, "since I'm awake now. I'll go straight back to sleep afterwards, I promise."

So she held Star, wrapped in a towel, and kept his neck very straight while Mum tube-fed him. Then she laid him back down in the pet carrier.

"Sleep well, Star," she whispered. "See you in the morning."

Star didn't move.

Jasmine tried to go to sleep, but worries started to creep into her mind. What if Star was still unconscious tomorrow? How long could he survive on nothing but glucose water? What if she looked in the box in the morning and he was –

No. She had to stay positive. Star was just dazed, and Mum was a really good vet. Star would be fine.

Chapter Five

He Seems Very Calm

Jasmine was woken by a strange scuffling sound. For a few seconds she lay in bed, confused. Then her eyes flew wide open.

Star!

She scrambled out of bed, crouched on the carpet next to the pet carrier and gently lifted the towel.

Star was standing up! As Jasmine lifted the towel, he gazed at her with dark intelligent eyes.

"Star, you're awake! And you've got such beautiful eyes!"

The little owl backed into the corner of the box.

"Poor thing. You're frightened, aren't you? Don't worry, I'm not going to hurt you. I'm so happy you're getting better."

Jasmine gently lowered the towel again and looked at her alarm clock. Half past six. Mum would probably be awake.

Mum wasn't awake, and she wasn't that pleased to be woken, either. But when Jasmine told her the good news about Star, she became a bit more cheerful.

"Take him downstairs and get his food ready," she said. "And make me a cup of tea, would you? I'll be down in a minute."

Jasmine carried Star's box carefully down to the scullery. By the time Mum appeared, she had made the tea and mixed the glucose solution.

"We need to be really careful how we handle him now," Mum said. "He might be defensive. I need to pick him up from behind, so as not to

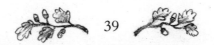

scare him. Can you lay that towel out, so we can wrap him up?"

While Jasmine did that, Mum took the other towel off the top of the pet carrier. Star was still standing in the corner with his eyes open.

"Oh, Jasmine," said Mum. "He really is beautiful, isn't he?"

Jasmine looked at the owl's amazing shiny black eyes in his extraordinary heart-shaped face. He looked wise and dignified and peaceful.

"He's *so* beautiful," she said. "Aren't you, Star?"

Mum opened the door behind Star, placed her gloved hands around his body and lifted him out. She wrapped him in the towel and handed him to Jasmine to hold while she tube-fed him.

"Now he's awake, should we give him proper food, too?" asked Jasmine.

"Definitely," said Mum, as she pushed the plunger down.

"Dog food?"

"No. Owls need raw meat. Chicken or beef.

There's a pack of mince in the fridge. Scoop
some into a saucer – about the amount it would
take to fill a matchbox."

Jasmine handed Star to Nadia while she
fetched the mince.

"Will he peck it up?" she asked.

"No, we'll have to feed him. If you hold his
beak open, I'll put the food in."

Jasmine sat down and held Star between her

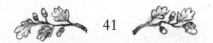

knees. She took the upper part of his beak and gingerly opened it. Star closed his eyes.

"That's right," said Nadia. "You can open it a bit wider."

She picked up a bit of mince about the size of her thumbnail and pushed it into the back of Star's mouth.

"Close his mouth now," she said, "and wait for him to swallow."

Jasmine let go of Star's beak. He opened and closed it a few times, moving his head backwards and forwards.

"Great," said Nadia. "He's swallowed it. We'll wait a few seconds for it to go down and then we can give him some more."

"When will he need his next feed?" asked Jasmine.

"Lunchtime," said Mum. "He needs feeding three times a day."

"So Dad will have to do it," said Jasmine. "Unless I have the day off school."

Mum smiled. "Nice try. But no. You'd better ask Dad very nicely. And I'll give him a crash course in owl-feeding."

Star kept his eyes closed while they fed him the rest of the mince, a tiny bit at a time.

"He seems very calm, doesn't he?" said Jasmine.

"He's still a bit dazed," said Mum. "But hopefully he'll be ready to go back into the wild by Sunday."

Sunday. Halloween.

"But it's Friday today," said Jasmine. "Can't we keep him a bit longer?"

Mum raised her eyebrows. "I'm not sure you'd enjoy feeding him so much after three days."

"Why not?"

"Well, owls eat every part of their prey. Meat alone won't give him the fibre he needs. So after three days you'd have to feed him chopped-up mice or chicks."

Jasmine pulled a face. "Oh. That's a bit gross."

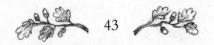

"Well, Sky should be fully recovered in a day or two, and then we can release him into the wild."

And, for once, Jasmine didn't argue with her mother.

Chapter Six
Top Secret

Jasmine took the Halloween party invitations
to school, hidden inside a book about Ancient
Egypt, which was their topic at the moment. On
the outside of each envelope was written:

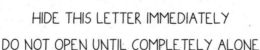

TOP SECRET!!!

HIDE THIS LETTER IMMEDIATELY

DO NOT OPEN UNTIL COMPLETELY ALONE

WARNING!!!

DO NOT UNDER ANY CIRCUMSTANCES OPEN AT SCHOOL

Jasmine spent most of the morning watching the fifteen people on the invitation list, waiting for them to be alone so she could slip them each an envelope without anyone else noticing.

By lunchtime, the only person who hadn't had their invitation was Aisha. When Jasmine and Tom finished eating, they went out to the playground to look for her. A big group of boys was playing football at the far end, and everyone else was in smaller groups.

"There she is, look," said Tom.

Aisha was talking to Harry, over in the corner by the fence.

"Ask Harry to go and play football with you," said Jasmine. "Then I can give Aisha the invitation."

"I can't do that," said Tom.

"Why not?"

"He'd think it was weird."

"What's weird about playing football?"

"You don't ask people to play. People just join

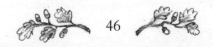

in if they want to."

"Well, think of something else, then."

As they drew closer, it became obvious that Aisha and Harry were having an argument.

"But you promised!" Aisha said.

Harry flung his hands out. "I can't help it, can I? It's not my fault if my parents decide things at the last minute."

"But we're going away straight after school today. What am I supposed to do with her?"

"I don't know. You'll have to ask someone else. Look, ask Tom."

"Ask me what?" said Tom.

Aisha gave Harry an exasperated look. "He promised he'd look after my hamster until Monday, and now he says he's going away too so he can't." She looked hopefully at Tom. "Would you like a hamster for the weekend?"

"Sorry," said Tom. "My mum can't stand rodents. She's only just got used to the guinea pigs, and she only allows them because

they live in the garden."

"I'll look after your hamster," said Jasmine.

Aisha stared at her. "Will you really?"

"Sure," said Jasmine. "I love hamsters. And me and Tom are going to have a boarding kennels when we grow up, to pay for our animal rescue centre, so we need experience of looking after all kinds of animals."

An image of Star came into her mind, and she suddenly had a worrying thought. A hamster would be food for an owl, wouldn't it?

But Star was in a cage, and the hamster would be in a cage too, so it wouldn't be a problem.

"That would be amazing," said Aisha. "Thanks so much, Jasmine. She's called Biscuit and she's so cute. Won't your parents mind, though?"

"Course not. They love animals," said Jasmine, sounding more certain than she really was. "Can you bring her round before five o'clock?"

It would be better if Biscuit arrived while Mum and Dad were out at work, Jasmine thought. She didn't want to ask their permission and risk them saying no. They might say she had enough animals to look after at the moment.

So it might be better to tell her parents about Biscuit later, once the hamster was already in the house and Aisha had gone away. Then they would have to agree to let her stay. They wouldn't have a choice.

Chapter Seven
Predator and Prey

"Oh, my goodness," said Jasmine. "It's huge!"

Aisha and her mum were standing on the doorstep. Beside them was the most enormous hamster cage Jasmine had ever seen. Inside was a complicated system of tubes and wheels and shelves and nest boxes. The base of the cage was filled with a deep layer of compost. The hamster was nowhere to be seen.

"Where's Biscuit?" asked Tom.

"She's in there," said Aisha, pointing to a nest box in the bottom corner. "She sleeps most of

the day, and then she wakes up in the evening and plays."

"Thank you, Jasmine," said Aisha's mum, and then she turned to Aisha and said something in Arabic. At least, Jasmine thought it must be Arabic, because she knew Aisha spoke Arabic at home.

"My mum says it's so kind of your parents to agree to have Biscuit at such short notice," said Aisha. "She says are they here? She'd like to thank them properly."

"Sorry," said Jasmine. "They're both at work."

Aisha translated this for her mother, who said something in reply.

"She says please thank them from her."

"I will. Come in."

Aisha's mum carried the cage into the house. Aisha followed with a bag of hamster food and a water bottle. Manu came out of the living room as they walked through the hall. His face lit up with excitement.

"What's in there?" he asked. "Have you got another animal?"

Jasmine's first reaction was to ignore her brother, but then she realised she would need him on her side. The last thing she wanted was Manu telling Mum and Dad about Biscuit as soon as they came home. She was going to have to find the right time to break the news, and she would have to choose her words very carefully.

"It's Aisha's hamster," she said. "I'm looking after her for a few days."

"Cool," said Manu. "Can I play with her?"

Aisha knew Manu from school. She gave him a suspicious look. "Only if you're really gentle. Hamsters get stressed if you don't handle them carefully."

"Of course I'll be gentle," said Manu, looking offended. "I do know how to handle animals, you know."

Jasmine snorted.

She led the way upstairs and opened the door

of her room, which she had hastily tidied when she got home from school.

"Biscuit can go in the corner there," she said, pointing.

Aisha's mum set the cage down.

"I cleaned it out yesterday," said Aisha, "so you won't need to. You can just take out any bits of dirty bedding, if you don't mind." She handed Jasmine a sheet of paper. "I wrote a list of when she needs feeding and everything."

"Thanks," said Jasmine, taking the list.

"What's in that cage?" asked Aisha, indicating the pet carrier.

"Oh, that's my owl."

Aisha's eyes widened. "You have an owl?"

"Well, he's not really mine. I found him by the wood. We think he flew into a window and knocked himself out. I'm looking after him until he's ready to go back into the wild."

"Will Biscuit be safe with an owl in the room?"

"Don't worry," said Jasmine. "We take him downstairs for feeding. He's always shut in his cage when he's up here."

"Can I see him?"

"Sure. He's called Star."

They knelt on the floor by Star's cage. Jasmine lifted the towel from the wire door. Star was standing in the middle of the cage with his eyes open. He raised his head and moved it from side

to side, all the time keeping his eyes fixed on the girls. Then he lunged his head forward and lowered his body right down to the floor. He spread his wings up and out and fluffed up his feathers to make himself look bigger.

"He's amazing," said Aisha. "He's so beautiful."

"He is, isn't he?" said Jasmine, her heart swelling with pride.

Star stopped moving, holding his pose as still as a statue.

"That's his defensive posture," said Jasmine, who had watched a video on the Barn Owl Trust website. "It means he's getting better."

Aisha's mum spoke to her in Arabic. "We need to go," Aisha said. "Thank you so much, Jasmine."

"It's a shame you'll miss our Halloween party," Jasmine said. "It's going to be amazing."

She waved them off from the front door. "Come on," she said to Tom. "Let's make some more decorations. Then we can play with Biscuit when she wakes up later."

They went back to Jasmine's room and she took out her craft things. But when she looked up, Tom was still standing in the doorway, frowning.

"What's wrong?" she asked.

"Do you think we should move Star to another room?" he said.

"Why?"

"Well, you know… We've got an owl and a hamster in the same room. It's kind of like predator and prey."

"But where else could we put Star? If he's downstairs, the cats might try to attack him. And there's no way I'm trusting Manu with him. Oh, that reminds me. I must tell Manu not to mention Biscuit. I need to tell Mum and Dad myself."

"We could put Star in Ella's room," said Tom. "She might not mind him. And she's quiet."

Jasmine shook her head. "When we have our rescue centre and boarding kennels, we'll be looking after all sorts of animals in the same place, won't we? They're both in their cages. It'll be fine."

Tom looked doubtful, but he didn't say anything.

"Let's make some snacks for Biscuit, so she feels at home," said Jasmine.

Tom picked up the sheet of instructions. "Aisha says she likes carrots and broccoli."

"That's easy, then. Mum always buys carrots and broccoli, even though I tell her not to. I bet there's some in the fridge."

They were cutting up a carrot when Mum walked into the kitchen. Jasmine froze, her knife poised over the chopping board.

"Hi, Mum," she said. "How was your day?"

"Fine, thank you," said Mum. "Why are you chopping carrots?"

"We were hungry," said Jasmine. "And you're always telling us to eat more healthy snacks."

"Well, yes," said Mum, "but I never expect you to take any notice. I'm very impressed, Jasmine. It's good to see that you're taking your parents' advice at last."

Chapter Eight
Where Is Biscuit?

Jasmine had planned to tell Mum and Dad about Biscuit during dinner. But Dad was stressed about some missing cattle passports, worrying about what would happen if the farm inspectors paid a surprise visit to check his paperwork. It probably wasn't the right time, Jasmine felt, to tell them she had another animal in her room.

After dinner, Tom brought Star's cage downstairs. When Jasmine lifted the towel and Star hunkered down in his defensive posture, Nadia smiled in delight.

"That's great! He's so much more alert. With any luck, he'll start feeding himself tomorrow, and then he'll be almost ready to go back into the wild."

Jasmine was going to tell Mum about Biscuit after they'd fed Star. But as Nadia watched him swallow the last piece of meat, her phone rang. She hastily laid him back in the cage.

"Can you close the cage door, Jasmine?" she called, as she stepped into the garden to answer the phone.

"Jasmine!" called Manu from the kitchen. "Can I play with the hamster?"

"Shh," hissed Tom.

Jasmine glanced fearfully towards Mum, but luckily she seemed absorbed in her phone call.

"Sorry," said Manu, as Tom and Jasmine came into the kitchen and shut the door behind them. "Why haven't you told them, anyway?"

"I'll tell them later, OK? You can come and play with Biscuit now if you like."

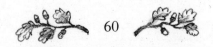

She put the towel back over Star's cage and carried it up to her room.

"Oh, look!" said Tom, as he opened Jasmine's bedroom door. "She's burrowing!"

Biscuit was digging a hole in the compost at the bottom of her cage, her front paws throwing up the earth with tremendous speed.

"That's so cool," said Manu. "I didn't know hamsters could dig."

"Jasmine!" called Mum from downstairs.

Jasmine went out on to the landing. "Yes?"

"I have to go and do emergency surgery on a dog. Dad's in the calf barn and Ella's in the kitchen if you need her. Where's Manu?"

"He's with us," said Jasmine. "See you later."

She went back into her room. "Let's take Biscuit out of her cage. I really want to cuddle her."

She opened the cage and scooped up the golden-haired hamster in both hands.

"Oh, she's so warm and soft."

Biscuit had bright black eyes, a twitchy pink nose and little rounded ears. She nestled in Jasmine's cupped hands and seemed very relaxed as Manu and Tom took it in turns to stroke her.

"Let's give her a snack," said Manu.

He took a piece of carrot from the cage and put it on the floor. Jasmine set Biscuit down in front of it. The hamster placed her little front paws on the carrot stick and started nibbling it with quick tiny bites.

"I bet her teeth are sharp," said Manu.

"Well, don't put your fingers near her mouth," said Jasmine.

"I won't," said Manu. "I'm not stupid."

Jasmine was about to make a cutting remark when Manu's eyes widened and his mouth dropped open. He silently raised his hand and pointed to something behind Jasmine.

Jasmine turned her head. Her heart stood still. There, standing on the carpet just outside the pet carrier, was Star.

63

Tom gasped and Manu yelped in fear as Star stretched himself tall. His huge wings spread out wide and then, flapping them, he rose straight up into the air. His eyes were locked on to the little hamster. In frozen horror, Jasmine saw Star's long legs stretch downwards, the steel-sharp talons pointed straight at Biscuit.

"NO!" she screamed. She dived to the floor, covering the hamster's body with her own, bracing herself for the pain of the owl's talons piercing into her back.

But there was nothing. Only the sound of Tom saying, "Thank goodness!"

Holding her breath, Jasmine raised her head. There above her was Tom, white-faced, holding a bundle in a blanket. She gaped at him.

"How did you do that?"

"I just grabbed the blanket off your bed and threw it over him," he said shakily.

"He was so quick," said Manu, wide-eyed and terrified. "He snatched the blanket and wrapped

it round Star just before he landed."

"It's lucky I was in time," said Tom. "He'd have really hurt you."

Jasmine shuddered at the memory of those outstretched talons heading straight towards her.

"How did he get out?" asked Manu.

Jasmine's stomach turned over as the horrible realisation came to her.

"It was my fault. I didn't shut the cage properly after we fed him. Mum told me to and then you came in and asked about the hamster and I just forgot to close the clips on the door. Oh, I'm so stupid!"

"We'd better put him back properly now," said Tom. He carried the blanket to the pet carrier. "I hope he's not injured."

He put the bundle in the carrier and gently took the blanket away before shutting the door and closing the clips. Star was standing up with his eyes closed.

"Is he asleep?" asked Manu.

"No, that's what they do when they're stressed," said Jasmine.

"I bet he's not as stressed as we are," said Tom.

Jasmine laughed shakily, a laugh that could easily have turned to tears. "I can't believe how stupid I am. Biscuit could have been killed and it would have all been my fault."

"It was just a mistake," said Tom. "And we saved Biscuit. That's the main thing."

"Where *is* Biscuit?" asked Manu.

Jasmine looked down at the place on the carpet where the hamster had been. The half-eaten carrot stick was still there. But there was no sign of Biscuit.

Chapter Nine
She Could Be Anywhere

The children stared at each other in horror. Manu scrambled to his feet and cast his eyes wildly around the room.

"Where is she?" asked Jasmine frantically. "She was right here. Where did she go?"

Tom's face was white. "She must be somewhere. She'll be hiding under some clothes or something." He started rummaging through a heap of Jasmine's discarded clothes on the floor. Jasmine watched him, paralysed with guilt and terror.

"You don't think ... Star did actually get her, do you?" she whispered.

"He can't have done," said Tom. "I grabbed him before he reached the floor."

Nevertheless, Jasmine lifted the blanket and peeped fearfully into Star's cage. Star had his eyes open now. He started to move his head from side to side as she looked at him.

There was nothing else in the cage. Thank goodness for that.

"Right," she said. "So Biscuit's safe, at least. We just need to find her."

Tom's face went even whiter. "The cats!"

Jasmine's eyes flew to the door, but it was firmly shut. "They're not in here. And they can't get in."

"But what if Biscuit goes downstairs?" said Manu.

"How could she?"

"Easily. She could squeeze under the door or go under the floorboards or anything."

"That's true," said Tom. "Hamsters can get

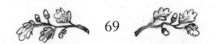

through tiny holes. She could be anywhere."

"Well, there's not much use saying that," said Jasmine. "How's that supposed to help?"

"Let's at least put the cats in the scullery," said Tom. "We can keep them shut in until we find Biscuit."

"They're probably there anyway," said Jasmine. "I'll go and check."

Sure enough, Toffee and Marmite were curled up together in their cosy basket on the scullery worktop. Jasmine closed the door and went back to her bedroom.

"We'll tell everyone to keep the cats in the scullery," she said. "We can say it's because we're worried they'll try to attack Star. I'll put a note on the door to remind everyone. They'll be fine in there. They can still go outside through the cat flap."

"Biscuit's probably still in this room," said Tom. "So let's look in all the places she's likely to be."

Manu crawled under the bed and started pulling out the boxes of toys. Tom lay down to look under the chest of drawers.

Jasmine had a sudden thought. "Maybe she went back in her cage."

"Yes!" said Tom. "That's the safest place, after all. I bet she's snuggled up in one of her nest boxes."

They looked in the nest boxes and the tubes, and Jasmine even dug around in the compost on the cage floor, in case Biscuit had burrowed down and covered herself completely. But they found nothing.

"Remember to look for hamster signs as well,"

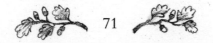

Jasmine said to Manu. "Droppings, and anything that's been chewed. Tom, can you help me move the wardrobe out so we can look behind it?"

They moved all the furniture and took everything out of the wardrobe and drawers, but there was no sign of Biscuit.

"Let's look in my room," said Manu. "She might have run in there."

By nine o'clock, they had searched every room except the kitchen. They were reluctant to go in there; it was never a good idea to interrupt Ella when she was working. But now they had no choice. Shooting each other glances of trepidation, they opened the door and tiptoed in.

"Go away," said Ella, without looking up from her textbook.

"Sorry," said Jasmine. "It's an emergency. We won't disturb you, honest."

"You've already disturbed me," said Ella.

Jasmine decided it was best not to say anything else. She dropped to her hands and knees and

started working her way around the edge of
the room, opening each cupboard as she went.
A mouse had got into one of the kitchen
cupboards once, so probably a hamster would be
able to find a way in too.

Tom was searching the other side of the
room. Manu crawled under the table and started
moving the chairs around, making a horrible
scraping sound.

Ella threw her pen on the table with a sound
like a frustrated tiger.

"Will you *please* get out? I need to
concentrate."

The door opened.

"What on earth are you all doing?"

It was Mum's voice.

Jasmine took her head out of the crockery
cupboard. Manu looked up from under the table.
Tom emerged from the broom cupboard. They
shot guilty glances at each other.

"We were playing a game," said Jasmine.

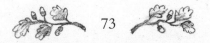

"We were looking for something," said Manu.

"Oh, yes?" said Mum. "What exactly were you looking for?"

Ella threw her hands up in frustration. "I don't care what they're looking for or what stupid game they're playing. Can you all please just get out of my room?"

"Your room?" said Mum. "This is the kitchen, Ella. Why don't you go and work in your own room if you want peace and quiet?"

"Fine," said Ella. "I'm going. Why aren't they in bed, anyway?"

"Ella, you were babysitting," said Mum. "You were meant to tell them to go to bed."

"There's no point. They don't take any notice of me."

"Go to bed, all of you," said Mum. "Tom, I'll come and make the camp bed up in a minute."

"Thank you," said Tom. But Jasmine's heart skipped a beat. Mum couldn't be allowed to come into her bedroom. Not with an enormous

hamster cage in the middle of the floor.

"Don't worry," she said. "We'll sort the bed out."

Mum looked at her in surprise. "Really?"

"Sure. You've had a busy day. You should sit down and rest."

Mum narrowed her eyes suspiciously. "What's going on, Jasmine?"

Jasmine's eyes widened in outraged innocence. "Just because I'm being kind and thoughtful, you think there's something going on? That's not very trusting."

Nadia smiled. "You're right. Thank you for sorting it out. Now, go and get ready for bed, all of you."

"That was lucky," muttered Manu, as they trooped upstairs.

"But we still haven't found Biscuit," said Tom.

Jasmine felt sick. How could she possibly tell Aisha that she'd lost her beloved hamster?

"She will come back, won't she?" said Manu.

"Course she will," said Jasmine. "When she gets hungry, she'll come back."

And she really, really hoped that was true. Because she had absolutely no idea what she would do if Biscuit didn't come back.

Chapter Ten
We Can't Tell Her Now

Jasmine draped a blanket over Biscuit's cage and threw lots of clothes over it.

"If Mum asks, I'll just tell her I'm in the middle of making her something for Christmas," she said. "Then she won't peek underneath it."

Tom looked doubtfully at the enormous blanket-covered cube. "What would you be making her that's that size?"

Jasmine shrugged. "I don't know. But I'm always making stuff. She won't suspect anything."

"Wouldn't it be easier just to tell her?" said

Tom. "All these secrets are stressing me out."

"I was going to," said Jasmine. "But we can't tell her now. She'd go mad if she knew I was looking after Biscuit without asking her *and* I'd nearly got her killed *and* now I've lost her."

"Mm," said Tom. "Yes, maybe it's best she doesn't know yet. Not until we've found Biscuit."

"Exactly. If we leave the cage door open and put food inside, maybe she'll come back tonight."

"I think we should put Star in another room," said Tom. "Biscuit might be able to smell him, and then she won't come back in here."

Jasmine looked at him thoughtfully. "You're right. But where?"

"We could put him in the dining room," said Tom. "And that will be an even better reason for everyone to keep the cats shut in the scullery. So it will work for Star *and* Biscuit."

"We can tell Mum we're worried he might keep us awake if he stays in my room," said Jasmine. "Since he's getting so much more lively."

Nadia laughed when they told her this. "Far more likely that you and Tom would keep *him* awake. But it's probably a good idea for him to be in a quiet room on his own. Hopefully he'll be able to feed himself by tomorrow, and then we can release him on Sunday."

When Jasmine woke up on Saturday morning, her first thought was Biscuit. But when she looked into the cage, the food was untouched. She checked every inch of the cage, but Biscuit wasn't there.

Tom sat up in bed as she was checking the last nest box.

"Not back?"

Jasmine shook her head. Her insides were twisted with worry.

"I don't know what to do. How can we get her back?"

"Let's look online," said Tom. "I bet there's stuff about how to find an escaped hamster."

There was. They were relieved to read that
they had done the right thing by leaving the
cage door open with food inside. They were
slightly reassured, too, to read that many hamsters
do return safely to their cages, sometimes after
several days. And they followed a tip to place
four sunflower seeds on the floor in
every room of the house, so they
could count them regularly to
check whether Biscuit was in a
particular room.

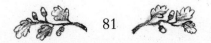

After breakfast, Nadia, Tom and
Jasmine went to feed Star. When Jasmine lifted
the towel from his cage, Star backed into the far
corner and went into full defensive posture. He
lunged his head forward, hunkered down as low
as he could go, spread his wings up, fluffed out
his feathers and swayed his head from side to side.
Then he stopped moving and held his pose very
still, his huge eyes staring out at them.

As Jasmine watched him, she was filled with

a strange mixture of affection, admiration and also another emotion, one that she had never felt about an animal before.

Fear.

Star was a bird of prey. And last night, when she had seen his spear-sharp talons heading straight for the little hamster, Jasmine had, for the first time, properly understood what that meant.

It was Star's instinct to hunt and kill.

Everything about him, from his silent flight to his super-sensitive hearing, was designed to make him a better hunter. He was beautiful, but he was also deadly.

Nadia smiled. "He's so much livelier. That's great to see."

"Shall we see if he's ready to eat by himself?" asked Jasmine.

"Yes. I'll hold him while you put the meat in."

Nadia put on her gloves and lifted Star out while Jasmine tipped the food on to the cage floor. Then Nadia put Star back.

"He probably won't eat it straightaway. Owls expect their prey to be moving, not lying still. But I think he'll work out that it's food eventually, if we leave him to it."

Jasmine and Tom decided to research barn owls while they were waiting.

"I can't believe how ugly the chicks are when they first hatch," said Tom, who was looking through Nadia's book on owls. "Can you believe

Star ever looked like that?"

"Oh, no!" said Jasmine.

"What?"

"Look. Star might have chicks to feed. It says the father brings food to the nest for up to fourteen weeks, and chicks can be born any time from March to August. So Star might have a family."

"We should go and look in the barn," said Tom, already getting to his feet. "See if we can find a nest."

"Wait," said Jasmine. "We should find out what we're looking for first."

They looked at pictures of barn owl nests, which weren't really nests at all, just piles of squashed droppings and pellets. They discovered that barn owls don't build nests, so they need to use a level surface, somewhere sheltered from rain and wind.

"It would be really cool to find owl pellets," said Tom. "Look, there's a chart here of all the animal bones that might be inside a pellet."

"Let's go up to the barn now," said Jasmine. "Imagine if we found Star's family!"

"We won't be able to have the party in the barn if owls are nesting there," said Tom.

Jasmine stared at him. She hadn't thought of this.

"No," she said. "We won't. But Star and his family are more important than the party."

Chapter Eleven
An Excellent Sign

Before they went to the barn, they checked on Star. He was standing in the corner of the cage with his eyes shut. All the mince had disappeared. Jasmine ran to the kitchen to tell Nadia.

"Come and look, Mum! He's eaten all the food by himself!"

"That's an excellent sign," said Nadia. "We just need to flight-test him now, make sure he's properly better. If he's flying well, we can release him tomorrow."

"How will we flight-test him? Won't he just fly away?"

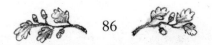

86

"We need to do it in an aviary," said Nadia. "The Heathfields have got one, up at Sheepfold Farm."

"What's an aviary?" asked Tom.

"It's an outdoor bird enclosure," said Nadia. "Big enough for birds to fly around in, but with chicken wire over the top and sides, so they can't get out. Mrs Heathfield used to keep golden pheasants in hers, but it's empty now. I'll give her a call."

⋆⭑

Tom and Jasmine took torches to search the barn. They couldn't see any sign of a nest among the roof beams, so they shone their torches over the floor to look for feathers, droppings and pellets.

Suddenly Tom said, "Look! Over here!"

Jasmine hurried over. Tom's torch beam lit up splashes of what looked like white paint.

"Barn owl droppings!" she said. "Exactly like the picture on the website."

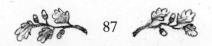

She shone her torch up to the roof beams. "I can't see anything that looks like a nest, though."

"No," said Tom, who was doing the same. "I think an owl is just roosting here, not nesting. There's no feathers around."

"And I don't think it's been a roost for very long," said Jasmine, "or there'd be a lot more droppings."

"There should be pellets somewhere," said Tom. "The book said owls cough up one or two pellets after each night's hunting."

But although they searched for a long time, they didn't find anything that looked like an owl pellet.

"That must mean the owl wasn't here for very long," said Jasmine. "If it was Star, maybe he never came back from his night's hunting because he crashed into the window."

"We should look at the window," said Tom. "See if there's any marks on it."

They retraced the path they'd taken through the brambles on Thursday evening, until they were standing under the window in the exact place where they'd found Star.

"That smudge in the dirt," said Tom, pointing. "Do you think that might be where Star hit the window?"

"It looks like it might be," said Jasmine.

"I hope he doesn't fly into another window once he's free again," said Tom. "That would be awful."

"We'll have to be really careful where we release him," said Jasmine. "Somewhere far away from any hazards."

Manu was disappointed that they hadn't found an owl pellet. "I wanted to dissect it," he said, "and find all the little skulls of the animals he'd eaten."

"You can buy owl pellets online," said Tom. "I'll get you one for your next birthday."

"Did you phone the lady with the aviary, Mum?" asked Jasmine.

"Yes, and she's very happy for us to do Star's flight test tomorrow. I arranged to go at eleven o'clock."

"I can't wait to see him fly," said Jasmine. "It'll be amazing. Can Tom come, too?"

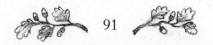

"Of course," said Nadia. "Oh, that reminds me, Tom. Your mum phoned to say she'll pick you up around five o'clock."

"So can we do some baking this afternoon?" asked Jasmine.

"If you like. What do you want to make?"

"Halloween cupcakes and biscuits. In case anyone comes trick-or-treating here."

"That's a nice idea," said Nadia. "Though I can't imagine anyone bothering to walk all the way up the farm track to come trick-or-treating. You might end up eating all the cakes yourselves."

"Oh, well," said Jasmine. "That wouldn't be so terrible."

Before they started baking, they checked Biscuit's cage and counted all the sunflower seeds. Nothing had been eaten and there was no sign of Biscuit.

"It doesn't seem right to have a party when Biscuit's still missing," said Jasmine.

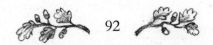

"I think she'll come back tonight," said Tom. "She's nocturnal, remember, so she's probably curled up asleep somewhere. Maybe she's under the floorboards in your room. You can listen out for her this evening."

"I will," said Jasmine. "And I'll make more Halloween decorations while I'm listening."

"Should we decorate the barn tomorrow morning, before Star's flight test?" asked Tom. "I can say I'm meeting you in the woods to walk Sky."

"Sure," said Jasmine. "And I'll bring Sky with me, so it won't even be a lie."

Chapter Twelve
The Flight Test

Jasmine checked the sunflower seeds twice more that day, but they were all still there. She checked Biscuit's cage again, but it was still empty.

She sat quietly in her bedroom all evening, cutting out silhouettes of owls and bats and spiders from black card, and threading them on lengths of cotton. She listened out the whole time for any sounds of Biscuit waking up and moving around. But she heard nothing.

Jasmine woke up on Sunday morning full of hope, but Biscuit still wasn't in her cage and the

fresh food was untouched.

She tried not to panic. There was still time.

Not much time, though. Aisha was coming
back tomorrow, and how could Jasmine possibly
face her if Biscuit hadn't been found by then?

How could she have been so stupid? If Manu
had left the cage door open, she would have
been absolutely furious with him.

Jasmine realised, with an unfamiliar feeling
of respect for her brother, that not once had
Manu told her she'd been stupid. And he hadn't
breathed a word to Mum and Dad, either.

She got dressed and put the Halloween
decorations and fairy lights in her backpack. As
she passed Manu's room on her way downstairs,
she saw him kneeling
on his floor building a
complicated Lego model.
It was impossible to tell
what it was. Manu never
followed the instructions;

he just made whatever he felt like making.

"I'm taking Sky for a walk," Jasmine told him. "Would you mind checking the sunflower seeds?"

"OK," said Manu, adding a pirate to his construction.

"And Manu?"

Manu gave the pirate a machine gun. "What?"

"Thanks for being so helpful with all this. And for not telling anyone."

Manu looked at her in surprise. "That's OK," he said.

Tom was walking towards the barn from the other direction as Jasmine arrived. She gave him the disheartening news about Biscuit.

"But Manu's checking the sunflower seeds," she said. "So you never know."

"Fingers crossed," said Tom.

He had brought all the things for the Halloween maze. "I cooked the spaghetti before

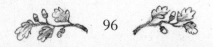

96

Mum and Dad woke up," he said proudly.

"It's going to be so creepy," said Jasmine. "I can't wait."

They were planning to blindfold the guests, two at a time, and lead them outside, where they would make them do things like handle a lump of cold spaghetti (brains), pick up peeled grapes (eyeballs) and put their hands in a bowl of ketchup (blood), while playing a soundtrack of eerie noises and telling them a story about a gruesome murder in the woods.

"It will be so scary," said Tom. "Noah will totally freak out."

The decorating took longer than they'd expected, especially as the decorations kept getting caught on cobwebs when they tried to throw them over the beams. But by the time they had finished, the barn was transformed. There were fairy lights looped up over every convenient nail in the walls, and bats, spiders and owls hanging from all the beams.

"It looks amazing," said Tom.

"Even better than I thought," Jasmine said. She checked her watch. "We'd better go."

"I can't wait to see Star fly," said Tom.

"Let's hope he can," said Jasmine. "I think he needs to be back in the wild as soon as possible." She laughed ruefully as a thought struck her. "It's funny, isn't it? Star's in a cage, but he really needs to be in the wild. And Biscuit's in the wild, but she really needs to be in a cage."

The aviary was actually a big orchard, with apple and pear trees growing in the long grass. The only thing that made it different from a normal orchard was that the whole space was enclosed by a high cage made of chicken wire.

They set Sky's carrying case down on the ground. They hadn't fed him today. He needed to be hungry so he would come back for food after his flight.

"Right," said Mum. "What we want is to see

him make a vertical take-off from the ground, and then fly strongly and evenly. And he needs to be able to land and balance on a swinging perch."

"Is there a swinging perch here?" asked Jasmine.

"A thin branch will be fine," said Mum. "We just need to check that his strength and balance are good enough for him to cope in the wild."

Jasmine took the towel from the cage. Star was standing facing her, his bright eyes wide open.

"We're going to watch you fly, Star," she said.

"Stand right back and be very quiet, you two," said Mum.

She put on her gloves, lifted Star out and set him on the ground. Jasmine held her breath.

Star stood completely still. A gentle breeze ruffled his wing feathers. He moved his head very slightly to the right. Watching. Listening.

Then he lowered his head, raised his wings and spread them high and wide above his body. He bent his legs and took off, his legs stretched out behind him, his wings spread in a great fan. He

flew close to the ground, flapping his wings a few times, then soared up and landed on a fence post on the other side of the aviary. His talons gripped the post and he tucked his wings in close to his body and stood upright again, turning his head slightly to take in his surroundings.

"Wow," whispered Jasmine. "He didn't make a sound."

Nadia was smiling. "He seems to be flying strongly. I'd just like to see him land in a tree if possible."

As they watched, Star lowered his body again, spread his wings and sprang into the air. He soared silently towards them and landed on a tree stump. He looked around enquiringly. Then he took off again and flew between the apple trees. He flapped his wings and soared

above the treetops. He swooped down and
landed in the topmost branch of the tallest tree.
The thin branch swayed slightly, but Star stayed
firmly upright, his talons wrapped tightly around
the wood.

"That's a swinging perch, right?" whispered
Jasmine.

"It definitely is," murmured Mum. "He's ready
to be released."

Chapter Thirteen
The Release Site

It took a while to get Star back in his cage. They put meat inside but he took no interest in it at first. He was clearly enjoying flying back and forth through the trees, landing on branches and posts and then taking off again.

Eventually, though, he swooped down to the cage door, walked inside and started to eat. Mum closed the door behind him and went to the farmhouse to thank Mrs Heathfield while Star finished his meal.

"Are we going to release him now?" asked

Tom, when Nadia returned.

"Not now, no. Owls need to be released at dusk, which will be about half past five today. It's lucky I'm not on call."

In the car, Jasmine gazed out of the window in silence, desperately hoping Biscuit would be back in her cage when they got home. Suddenly she frowned and leaned forward. Nadia had driven right past the entrance to the farm.

"Mum? Where are we going?"

"I thought we'd have a look at the release site. I want to check that there aren't any hazards that might harm Star. It will be too dark to check this evening."

"What do you mean? What release site?"

"The barn where you found him," said Mum. "It's very important to release an owl at the same place you found it."

Jasmine gasped. "No!"

Nadia glanced at her in the rear-view mirror. "What's wrong?"

Jasmine and Tom shot each other fearful looks.

"It's just … the barn is where he was injured," said Jasmine. "It wouldn't be fair to release him there. What if he flies into the window again?"

"That's why I want to check it out," said Nadia. "If I think the window is what harmed him, I'll phone the owner and ask permission to board it up."

"But…" said Jasmine, desperately searching for a way out of this horrific situation. "I think the barn's haunted."

Nadia burst out laughing. "Oh, come on, Jasmine. I know it's Halloween, but really!"

"It is, though," said Jasmine. "When Tom and I were up there the other night we heard all these really spooky noises. Didn't we, Tom? And somebody died in that barn once, and everyone says his ghost comes out at Halloween."

Nadia shook her head. "That's complete rubbish and you know it. Honestly, Jasmine, you are ridiculous sometimes."

She parked the car at the entrance to the field.

"We'll release Star outside the barn, won't we?" said Tom. "Not inside?"

"Outside, yes," Nadia said. "Come on, you two. Let's go and have a look around."

There weren't any decorations on the outside of the barn, Jasmine reassured herself. They would just have to make sure Mum didn't go inside. And there was no reason why she would. Was there?

"What a perfect location for barn owls," said Nadia, looking at the dilapidated old building. "Can you show me exactly where you found him?"

"It was over here," said Jasmine. "Look. That's where he was lying."

"I'm impressed you spotted him in all this undergrowth," said Nadia.

"It was only because he was so white. I thought he was a plastic bag or something."

"See that smudge in the dirt?" Tom said to Nadia, pointing to the window. "Do you think that's where Star crashed into the glass?"

"I think it's very likely," said Nadia. "I'll ask the owner if I can board it up."

"So shall we go now?" asked Jasmine. The sooner they got Mum away from here, the better.

"Why are you in such a hurry?" asked Nadia. "I want to have a look around for any other hazards. I'd have thought you'd want to make sure Star had the best possible chance of a safe release."

"I do," said Jasmine, guiltily. "Of course I do."

"Are there any other windows?" Nadia asked.

"No," said Tom. "Only this one."

"Are you sure?" She was heading towards the barn door.

"There aren't," said Jasmine. "Honestly. We checked."

"I'd like to have a look inside anyway," said Nadia. "In case there are any other potential hazards."

 108

Jasmine shot Tom a desperate look. Mum was almost at the door.

"I wonder if –" Nadia began. And then she stopped dead in the doorway.

Nobody moved. Nobody spoke. Jasmine felt as though something was squeezing her chest and stopping her from breathing. The silence was unbearable.

Slowly, Nadia turned to face the children. "Jasmine?"

Jasmine didn't dare look at her. She kept her eyes on the ground. She said nothing. What could she say?

Nadia stepped inside the barn. "Jasmine. Tom. Come in here, please. I think you've got some explaining to do."

Chapter Fourteen
Quite a Bit of Trouble

Nadia stood in the centre of the barn, her eyes roaming left and right, up and down. From the silhouetted creatures hanging from the beams to her Christmas lights strung along the walls. From the bottle of ketchup to the tub of peeled grapes to the tangle of cooked spaghetti. And finally, back to Tom and Jasmine, standing at the doorway in petrified silence.

"I'm waiting," she said.

But Jasmine's mind was frozen as well as her body. She could think of absolutely nothing

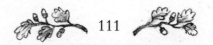

to say. Tom wasn't saying anything either. And Mum was just standing there. Waiting.

After what seemed like forever, Mum said, "You told me you were meeting some friends this evening to go trick-or-treating."

"We are," said Jasmine.

"So what's all this for, then?"

"We thought it would be nice to decorate the barn for Halloween."

"Just for the two of you?"

"Yes," said Jasmine, her insides squirming.

"You've gone to quite a bit of trouble, haven't you? You must have spent some time making all these decorations. And finding my Christmas lights."

"Yes," muttered Jasmine.

"And making all those cupcakes and biscuits. Enough for quite a lot of people, I would think."

Jasmine said nothing.

"And taking Sky for that long walk in the woods this morning? I did wonder why you took a

backpack with you. And I also wonder
why you didn't mention any of this to me."

Nadia's phone started to ring. She gave Jasmine
a steely look as she took it out of her pocket.

"Don't move," she said.

Jasmine hoped it would be a call about an
animal. Nothing too serious, obviously, but
something that Mum would have to rush off to
immediately and that would take a long time. So
long, in fact, that when she came back she would
have forgotten all about the decorated barn.

"Really?" said Nadia to the person on the
phone. She gave Jasmine an even steelier glare.
"How interesting. And what did this top-secret
invitation say, exactly?"

Jasmine's stomach plummeted. Tom clenched his
fists. This was it. Nothing could save them now.

As Nadia listened to the caller, her expression
grew grimmer by the second.

"I'm so sorry," she said. "Yes, you're absolutely
right. Incredibly irresponsible. And potentially

dangerous, as you say. Yes, it is lucky you found out in time. As a matter of fact, Karen, I've just found out myself, so I would have phoned you any minute now if you hadn't beaten me to it. I've got Jasmine right here, and I'm going to put her on the line to apologise in person."

Jasmine stared at her mother in horror.

"It's Noah's mum," Nadia said, handing her the phone. "I think you'd better grovel, don't you?"

Jasmine thought nothing could be worse than apologising to Noah's angry mother. But she was wrong.

When she handed the phone back, the only thing Mum said was, "I'm so furious I can't even speak to you right now." And she kept her word. The journey home was completely silent.

When they got home, Mum handed Jasmine a sheet of paper and a pen.

"Write down the name of everyone you've invited to this secret party," she said.

With a glance of despair at Tom, Jasmine silently wrote down all the names. She handed the list to Mum.

"*Fifteen* people!" said Nadia. "You were planning to host a party for fifteen children in a dangerously dilapidated farm building – a building that doesn't even belong to us, by the way – in the middle of nowhere, without any of those children's parents having a clue where they were! Honestly, Jasmine, I don't even know what to say."

Her face looked tighter and tenser than Jasmine had ever seen it. She went to the fridge and took down the class list of addresses and phone numbers.

"You're going to phone the parents of every child you've invited, and explain exactly what you were planning to do and why it's all cancelled. And then you'll have to hand the phone to me so I can apologise too. And by the end of all that, I hope you'll have realised exactly why your secret Halloween party was such a stupid idea."

Chapter Fifteen
Surprise!

The following hour was the worst of Jasmine's entire life. Even if she lived to be a hundred, she thought, nothing in her future could ever be as bad as that.

And then, just as she finished the last hideous phone call, the doorbell rang.

"That'll be Tom's mum," said Nadia. "You can invite her in and apologise in person."

With a sinking heart, Jasmine opened the door. She had already had to explain everything to Tom's mum over the phone, and Mel had not been at all happy.

But it wasn't Mel on the doorstep.

It was Aisha and her mum.

"Surprise!" said Aisha.

Jasmine stood rooted to the spot.

"But… But you said… " she stammered. "I thought… You said Monday… It's Sunday."

"We came home early," said Aisha. "So we thought we'd collect Biscuit now, if that's OK."

Jasmine made a huge effort to seem normal. "Yes, of course," she said, with a big fake smile.

"Jasmine!" called Mum. "Don't leave Mel on the doorstep."

Jasmine pulled herself together. "The problem is," she whispered urgently to Aisha, "I still haven't quite got round to telling my mum about Biscuit. So would you mind … you know … not mentioning it?"

Aisha pulled a face. "That's awkward. Why should I say I'm here, if I'm not collecting Biscuit?"

"Also," Jasmine whispered, "she's found out

about the Halloween party and she's really mad at me."

"Oh, great," said Aisha. "Even more awkward."

"Hi, Mel!" called Nadia, opening the door from the kitchen. She looked surprised for a moment, and then she smiled. "Oh, hello, Aisha. Hi, Rana."

"Aisha and her mum are here about the Halloween party," said Jasmine, giving Aisha a meaningful look.

"Oh, are they?" said Nadia. She gave Rana a strained smile. "You'd better come in."

Manu was sitting at the kitchen table next to Tom, drawing skeletons. When Aisha walked in, the boys' eyes opened wide in shock. Jasmine knew they were thinking exactly the same as she was. How on earth were they going to deal with this situation?

"I'm so very sorry about the party," said Mum. "I hope Jasmine has apologised profusely."

Rana said something to Aisha in Arabic.

Jasmine remembered the phrase from the other evening. She was pretty sure Rana was thanking Nadia for looking after the hamster. Thank goodness Mum didn't understand Arabic.

"My mum says thank you so much for inviting me to the Halloween party," said Aisha. "She says it was very kind of Jasmine and Tom to organise a party."

Jasmine looked at her friend in gratitude. She was certain Aisha's mum hadn't said anything of the sort. Good old Aisha.

Aisha's mum smiled at Nadia. "Thank you," she said in English.

"Oh," said Mum, looking a bit taken aback. "Well, yes, I suppose it was kind. It's just a shame they didn't think of asking permission beforehand."

Rana spoke to Aisha again. It was all in Arabic, except for one word at the end. "Biscuit."

Nadia looked puzzled.

"Er, should we come back tomorrow instead?"

Aisha asked Jasmine.

"Yes, please," said Jasmine. "Thank you."

Nadia looked curiously from Jasmine to Aisha and back again.

Aisha turned to her mum and was half way through a sentence when Manu shouted, "Biscuit!"

Everyone turned and stared at him. Tom and Jasmine's eyes darted frantically around the room.

"Where?" asked Jasmine.

"Manu, why are you shouting?" asked Mum. "If you want a biscuit, you can ask nicely."

"Sorry," said Manu. "Please may I have a biscuit?"

Mum tutted and opened the cupboard where she kept the biscuits. As soon as her back was turned, Manu pointed frantically to the corner of the room, where there was a little hole in the skirting board.

"She was there," he mouthed at Jasmine. "And

then I don't know where she went."

"What?" said Aisha, who unfortunately had been looking at Manu too. "Who was there?"

Then she gasped and her eyes opened very wide. "No! Have you lost Biscuit?"

Mum stood up, holding an empty tin. She gave Aisha a funny look.

"I haven't lost the biscuits, but it appears that *somebody*," she said, glaring at Manu, "has decided to help themselves to the entire tin."

Manu's face was a picture of wounded innocence. "Why do you always think it's me?"

"Because it *is* always you."

"That's not fair. It wasn't me who lost Biscuit."

"What is this about losing biscuits? The biscuits aren't lost. They've been eaten."

"Well, this one *nearly* got eaten," said Manu, giving Jasmine a meaningful stare, "and then *somebody* lost it."

"What's happened to Biscuit?" asked Aisha. "Will somebody tell me what's going on?"

"Will somebody tell *me* what's going on?" said Mum. "I'm completely confused."

Rana turned to Aisha and started talking very fast in Arabic. Aisha interrupted her. Everybody started talking at once.

Suddenly another voice cut through the chaos.

"Sorry for walking in, Nadia, but the door was open."

It was Tom's mum, with a very strained look on her face.

"Sorry," she said again. "It looks like you're busy here. Hello, Aisha. Hello, Rana. Tom, fetch your things and we'll get out of Nadia's way. You've caused quite enough trouble for one day. I'm so sorry, Nadia. I'm absolutely mortified."

"Oh, honestly, Mel, please don't apologise," said Nadia. "If I know anything about my daughter, I can bet she was the one behind all this."

"I'm sure Tom was just as much involved as Jasmine was," said Mel. "Come on, Tom, we're

going home. Put your shoes on."

She picked up a pair of trainers from the floor.

"AAARGHH!!"

She dropped them as though they were red-hot coals. One landed on the floor and the other on the table.

Everyone stared, open-mouthed, as Mel stepped back from the shoe on the table as though it was a ticking bomb. She pointed a trembling finger at it.

"In there," she whispered. "In there. A… a … a *rodent*."

Everybody's eyes turned to Tom's trainer. Nobody spoke. Nobody moved.

And then a little pink nose and a set of white whiskers popped up from the tongue of the shoe, followed by the cutest little face with bright black curious eyes.

Mel shrieked and clutched Jasmine's arm. "A rat!"

"A hamster!" said Nadia in wonder.

"Biscuit!" said everybody else.

"Biscuit! You're back!" said Jasmine. "Oh, thank goodness!"

Aisha scooped the little hamster out of the shoe, cupped her gently in her hands and kissed the top of her head.

"Come on, Biscuit," she said. "Let's take you home."

★⁎

"I'm so, so sorry, Aisha," said Jasmine, as Rana put Biscuit's cage in the car. "I'm so sorry we let her escape. I wouldn't blame you if you hated me forever."

"It wasn't your fault," said Aisha.

"But it was. It was completely my fault."

"Don't worry," said Aisha. "I'm just glad she's back. It's always awful when she escapes."

Jasmine stared at her. "She's escaped before?"

"Twice before. Once we found her in the garden, and once she was gone for days and then she just turned up in her cage again. So don't feel bad about it. She just likes escaping. Don't you, Biscuit?"

"I wish I could escape, don't you?" said Jasmine to Tom. "I'd rather live under the floorboards for the rest of my life than go back in that kitchen and face our mums."

Tom shuddered. "They were seriously mad before they found out about Biscuit. I can't even imagine what they're going to do to us now."

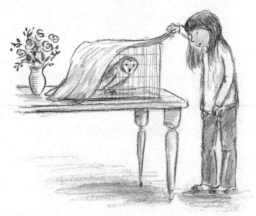

Chapter Sixteen

Happy
Halloween

"So I'm basically going to spend the whole
of half term being a slave to my family," said
Jasmine to Tom on the phone an hour later.
"Fetching in the logs, emptying the dishwasher,
laying *and* clearing away the table for every meal,
hoovering the house. I might as well be called
Cinderella."

"I'm not allowed any TV or games the whole
week," said Tom. "She's hidden all the remotes
and controllers."

"And no Halloween," said Jasmine. "Stuck

indoors on our own while everyone else goes out trick-or-treating and having parties."

"What about releasing Star?" asked Tom. "Is your mum going to take him on her own?"

"I don't know. She was so mad I didn't dare ask. But it will be so unfair if we don't get to be there, when it was us who found him."

"I know," said Tom. "And I won't even get the chance to say goodbye to him."

Jasmine spent the whole afternoon doing chores. Over the next few hours, her anger at her parents gradually turned into anger at herself. It had been a stupid idea to plan a secret Halloween party. What had she been thinking? Somebody's parents were bound to have found out sooner or later, even if Mum hadn't seen the decorations in the barn. How had she ever imagined they would get away with it?

And why hadn't she told her parents about Biscuit straightaway? They would have been annoyed at first, but they would have understood it was an emergency, and they wouldn't really have minded her looking after a hamster for a few days. Why had she kept it secret?

But then Biscuit had escaped, of course, and that was a whole different matter. Her parents wouldn't have been very amused about that. No, on reflection, she was actually quite glad she hadn't told them.

By the time it started to get dark, Mum still hadn't mentioned Star's release, and Jasmine's anger had been replaced with an overwhelming sadness. She would probably never again in her life get the chance to look after a barn owl, and now she wasn't even going to be there to say goodbye to him.

She hoovered the final corner of the living room and turned off the vacuum cleaner. She walked into the dining room and lifted the towel on Star's cage. Star looked at her for a moment before hunkering down in his defensive posture.

Jasmine looked at his bright intelligent eyes in his amazing heart-shaped face. She looked at his pure white chest and his beautiful wing feathers, silver and gold speckled with black-and-white spots. She looked at his hooked beak and his powerful feet with their deadly talons.

"Goodbye, Star," she said. "It's been amazing getting to know you. I hope you have a lovely life."

Star was in full defensive posture now. Jasmine lowered the towel and turned away from the table with tears in her eyes.

Mum was standing in the doorway. She didn't look angry any more.

"I'm going to take him up to the barn and release him now," she said.

"OK," said Jasmine.

"Do you want to come?" asked Mum.

Jasmine stared at her. "Really?"

Mum gave her a little smile. "I'm still really cross with you," she said. "But I think a week's worth of housework will probably teach you not to do

anything like that again, don't you?"

"Yes," muttered Jasmine.

"And I think the incident with Star and Biscuit taught you a lesson, too, about being extremely careful when handling animals with killer instincts."

"Yes," said Jasmine.

"And since you and Tom were the ones who rescued Star, I think it's only fair that you should both be there for his release."

"Oh, thank you, Mum," said Jasmine. "Thank you so much."

Once they had collected Tom, Mum parked the car in the gateway and they set off across the field. It was a beautiful evening, mild and still. A huge full moon hung low in the sky, and a few little stars had already come out.

As they walked past a heap of dead leaves, there was a rustling sound in the centre of it. They glanced at each other, stopped and waited.

More rustling sounds. Then a shiny black nose poked through the leaves, followed by a furry brown snout and a pair of bright black eyes.

A hedgehog!

The hedgehog clambered out of the leaf pile and snuffled about for a minute. Then it took a big handful of leaves in its mouth and pattered off into the hedge with them.

"It's making a nest to hibernate in," whispered Mum.

They waited for a couple of minutes but the hedgehog didn't return.

"Come on," whispered Mum. "Let's not disturb it."

"How lovely to see a hedgehog in the wild," said Jasmine, as they walked across the field. "I've never seen one before."

"Listen," said Tom. "Was that an owl?"

From somewhere across the field came an unmistakeable "toowit-toowoo" sound.

"A tawny owl," said Jasmine. "They're the only owls that make that sound."

An answering "toowit-toowoo" came from the wood. "And there's its friend," said Tom.

As they drew near to the barn, Jasmine jumped as a black silhouette flitted in front of them.

"A bat," whispered Tom.

"I expect they roost in the barn," said Mum. "It's a perfect place for bats."

Another black silhouette flitted across the field. Jasmine watched the barn entrance and saw another bat dart out, then another and another.

"They're going out hunting," said Mum. "I expect they're trying to eat as many insects as they can before they start hibernating."

She set Star's carrying case down a few metres away from the barn. Jasmine lifted the towel off the cage and crouched down beside it.

"Do you remember this place, Star? This is where we found you."

"Oh!" said Tom, turning to Nadia. "You did the window."

Jasmine looked, and saw that the window had been boarded up with a piece of wood.

"I phoned the owner and he said it was fine," said Nadia, "so I came up this afternoon and nailed it on. I didn't want to do it with Star here, in case the sound of hammering freaked him out."

Jasmine gazed at her mum in admiration. She might get a bit angry for no real reason sometimes, but she was quite amazing really, the way she took so much trouble with all the animals in her care.

"Thanks, Mum," she said.

"No problem," said Mum. "You two had better say your goodbyes to Star now, I'm afraid."

Tom crouched down next to Jasmine.

"Goodbye, Star. It's been amazing to spend time with you. I hope you have a great life in the wild. And try not to eat all the bats."

"Enjoy your freedom, Star," said Jasmine. "Maybe we'll see you again one evening, when you're out hunting. We'll look for you every Halloween. And every night when the stars come out, I'll think of you, flying among them."

Mum put on her gloves and opened the cage door. Holding his wings firmly against his body, she wrapped her hands around the owl and lifted him out. She set him gently on the ground, facing away from the barn, and stepped back.

They all stood still and silent, watching Star. He stood completely still, too. Only his feathers moved, ruffled by the breeze.

Star turned his head to one side, then the

135

other. Then he dipped his body down close to the
ground and lifted his wings. He stretched them
out to their full span and took off, skimming
horizontally over the long grass. Jasmine watched,
awestruck, as Star soared across the field in silent
flight, his white-and-silver body ghostly in the
moonlight. As he disappeared into a cluster of trees
on the other side of the field, an eerie screech was
carried back on the breeze.

"Goodbye, Star," whispered Jasmine. "You're amazing."

Mum leaned over and squeezed her shoulder. Then she picked up the cage and they headed back across the field.

For a few minutes, nobody spoke. Then Tom said, "That was the best Halloween ever."

Mum laughed.

"I mean it," said Tom. "We got to see a hedgehog, and bats, and watch a real ghost owl fly into the wild. No one else will have had a Halloween like that."

Nadia gave him an affectionate smile. "You're right, Tom. That was a unique Halloween."

"And we both have a black cat to go home to," said Jasmine.

"The best black cats in the world," Tom agreed.

"And Dad's making soup for supper," said Nadia. "And, thanks to you two and your cancelled party, there are plenty of Halloween cakes to eat. Even Manu can't have finished them all yet."

Jasmine felt immensely cheered up all of a sudden. "You're right, Tom," she said. "This really is the best Halloween ever."

Acknowledgements

Thank you to the Barn Owl Trust for their wonderfully informative website, and special thanks to Matthew from the Trust, who generously took the time to answer all my questions.